This is the day the LORD has made;
We will rejoice and be glad in it.

Psalm 118:24

THIS IS THE DAY!

written by
Amy Parker

illustrated by
Leeza Hernandez

Little Shepherd Books · New York
An Imprint of Scholastic Inc.

Wake up! Wake up!

Up, up, and away!

Let's rejoice and be glad —

God created this day —
He made it for YOU!
And He filled it with things
Just for YOU to do!

Don't dilly;
Don't dally —
Take this gift and run!

Don't dawdle;
Don't tarry —

Let's go have some fun!

There are teeth to brush and

Clothes to try,

OOF!

Hair to comb and

Shoes to tie!

There are plays to play . . .

And rockin' rides to ride!

When you're done with all that,
What else will you do?

You just never know what
Is waiting for you!

No matter the weather —

Sun, snow, rain, or gray,

You can still make it count —

Yes! This is THE day!

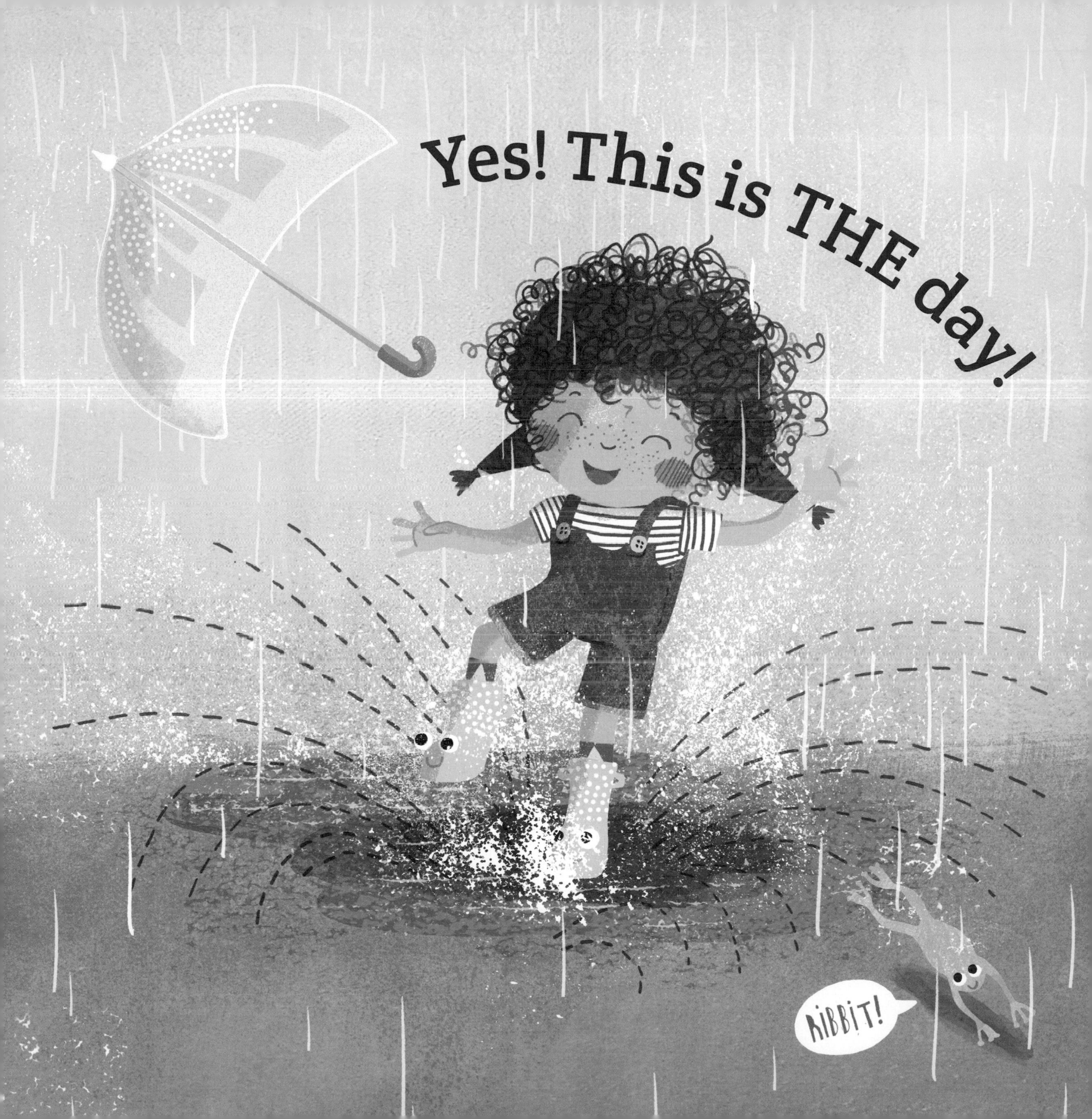

Feeling topsy-turvy?
Or angry or sad?

You can *still* make this day
The best that you've had!

When it's dark or scary,

GULP!

Stand tall and be brave.

You can smile your big smile,

And wave a big wave.

Don't give up! Don't give in!
Let God show you how!

Remember, He's got this —
No stopping you now!

Then when all is happy
And bubbly and bright,

Find that person who needs

God's bright-shining light.

When you take all that joy
And spread it around,

You make this world better!
You make it go 'round!

Make every second count.
Soak up every bit!

And when the day is done,
You'll be proud of it!

Right now is the moment.
It's yours! Don't delay!
Step into the sunshine!

Yes! This is THE day!

To Daniel:
You are the sun streaming through my window each day.
And to YOU:
If you have ever felt let down, left behind, or less than,
this book is for you. And this is YOUR day.
— A.P.

To Sheri, for her beautiful spirit and for being
one of the bravest women I know!
— L.H.

Text copyright © 2018 by Amy Parker
Illustrations copyright © 2018 by Leeza Hernandez

Scripture taken from the New King James Version®. Copyright © 1982 by Thomas Nelson.
Used by permission.

Library of Congress Control Number: 2016047097

ISBN 978-1-338-04703-5

10 9 8 7 6 5 4 3 2 1 • 18 19 20 21 22

Printed in China 38
First edition, April 2018
Book design by Jess Tice-Gilbert